SIMON AND SCHUSTER & NICKELODEON PRESENT:

EXTREME RESCUE

CROCODILE MISSION

| ERICA DAVID | WARNER MCGEE |
| writer | artist |

DORSET COUNTY LIBRARY

205239525 X

D0192040

GO!

DORSET COUNTY
COUNCIL

205239525 X

PETERS   £3.99

26-Jul-2010

BASED ON THE TV SERIES GO, DIEGO, GO! AS SEEN ON NICK JR.

First published in Great Britain in 2010 by Simon & Schuster UK Ltd • 1st Floor, 222 Gray's Inn Road, London WC1X 8HB • Originally published in the USA in 2009 by Simon Spotlight, an imprint of Simon & Schuster Children's Division, New York. • © 2010 Viacom International Inc. All rights reserved. NICKELODEON, Nick Jr., Go Diego, Go!, and all related titles, logos and characters are trademarks of Viacom International Inc. • All rights reserved including the right of reproduction in whole or in part in any form. • A CIP catalogue record for this book is available from the British Library
ISBN 978-1-84738-789-9 • Printed in China • 10 9 8 7 6 5 4 3 2 1

Visit our websites: www.simonandschuster.co.uk www.nickjr.co.uk

DEEP IN THE SWAMP NEAR A GIANT RIVER, DIEGO AND HIS FRIEND BABY JAGUAR WALKED THROUGH THE SOFT, MARSHY GROUND. THEY WERE LOOKING FOR CROCODILES! ¡LOS COCODRILOS!
I LIKE CROCODILES, DIEGO, BUT SOMETIMES THEIR SHARP TEETH MAKE THEM LOOK SCARY.
YOU HAVE SHARP TEETH TOO, BABY JAGUAR.
OH, YEAH!
CROCODILES DO HAVE SHARP TEETH, BUT THAT'S SO THEY CAN EAT MEAT.

DIEGO WALKED DEEPER INTO THE SWAMP. HE CAREFULLY PICKED HIS WAY THROUGH THE BRANCHES AND VINES THAT BLOCKED HIS PATH. AFTER A WHILE HE FOUND HIMSELF WALKING DOWN A STEEP SLOPE.
WITHIN MINUTES THE SKY GREW DARK AND IT STARTED TO RAIN.
THE GROUND IS GETTING REALLY MUDDY. I'D BETTER BE CAREFUL!
THE RAIN POURED DOWN FROM THE DARK CLOUDS OVERHEAD. DIEGO HEARD A RUMBLING NOISE THAT SOUNDED LIKE THUNDER. BUT WHEN HE LOOKED BEHIND HIM, HE REALISED IT WASN'T THUNDER AT ALL.
IT'S A MUDSLIDE!

THE WALL OF MUD OOZED DOWN THE SLOPE AFTER DIEGO!

THE RAIN DIDN'T LAST MUCH LONGER, AND SOON THE SUN CREPT OUT FROM BEHIND THE CLOUDS. FROM THE TOP OF THE TREE, DIEGO COULD SEE THE ENTIRE SWAMP BELOW.
WHAT A VIEW! I CAN USE MY SPOTTING SCOPE TO FIND THE LITTLE CROCODILE.
DIEGO HELD THE SPOTTING SCOPE UP TO HIS EYE.
THERE'S THE CROCODILE OVER IN THAT STREAM!
I'VE GOT TO HURRY!
I CAN GET THERE QUICKLY BY SWINGING THROUGH THE TREES.

IF WE STAND VERY STILL AND LISTEN CAREFULLY, MAYBE YOU CAN HEAR YOUR FAMILY AT THEIR NEW HOME.
LET'S TRY IT!